JENNY GIRAFFE'S
MARDI GRAS
❧ RIDE ❧

Cecilia Casrill Dartez

JENNY GIRAFFE'S
MARDI GRAS
❧ RIDE ❧

Illustrated by Andy Green

PELICAN PUBLISHING COMPANY
GRETNA 2012

First printing, January 1997
Second printing, September 2002
Third printing, August 2008
Fourth printing, October 2012

*To all lovers of Mardi Gras everywhere . . .
in the past, present, and future.*

My heartfelt, sincere appreciation to all of the following who have helped Jenny on to another fun-filled adventure: the wonderful super-krewe Orpheus, for their special permission; to a truly dedicated Mardi Gras man, Arthur Hardy; for the special permission from the enthusiastic and devoted Blaine Kern's Mardi Gras World; and to dear Nina Kooij, a truly dedicated editor.

---

*The word "Pelican" and the depiction of a pelican are trademarks
of Pelican Publishing Company, Inc.,
and are registered in the U.S. Patent and Trademark Office.*

Library of Congress Cataloging-in-Publication Data

Dartez, Cecilia Casrill.
    Jenny Giraffe's Mardi Gras ride / Cecilia Casrill Dartez ;
illustrated by Andy Green.
        p. cm.
    Summary: While preparing for her ride in one of the super Mardi Gras parades, Jenny Giraffe discovers the tradition of float riders, masks, and costumes.
    ISBN-13: 978-1-56554-182-5 (hardcover : alk. paper)
    [1. Mardi Gras—Fiction. 2. Parades—Fiction. 3. Giraffes-
-Fiction.] I. Green, Andy, ill. II. Title.
    PZ7.D258Jg 1996
    [Fic]—dc20
                                                    96-27300
                                                    CIP
                                                    AC

Printed in Singapore

Published by Pelican Publishing Company, Inc.
1000 Burmaster Street, Gretna, Louisiana 70053

JENNY GIRAFFE'S MARDI GRAS RIDE

Jenny had just completed her steamboat painting, and she was quite proud. So as she packed her bag to go home, she wondered about the surprise treat that Claude and Angelle had planned.

However, it was as just as she started to walk home that she saw them.
Purple! Green! Gold!

Beautiful decorations with all these colors were on balconies, doors, and windows and everywhere on houses and apartments.

Of course, a very curious Jenny wondered, "Why are there so many decorations in all the same colors?"

When she went inside, her family and friends were waiting with a special ring-shaped cake. "Those colors again!" she exclaimed. "And . . . what kind of funny cake is that?"

"It's a King Cake, Jenny, and this is your first King Cake party!" said Lita. "In the King Cake somewhere, there's a little plastic baby. Whoever gets it has to have the next party."

Claude then cut the cake.

"I got it!" yelled T-Boy. He held up the tiny plastic doll, and then placed the cardboard crown on his head.

"Lita, will you be the queen for my King Cake party?" he asked as he made a deep bow.

"*De*-lighted!" said Lita, trying to sound very grown-up.

Now Jenny was bursting with curiosity. "Why do we have King Cake parties, and why are the purple, green, and gold colors everywhere in our neighborhood?"

Claude then told her that King Cake parties begin on January 6, King's Day. This day reminds us of the journey of three kings who brought gifts to the newborn Christ child many years ago.

Our Carnival season begins on King's Day, and the last day of the season is called "Mardi Gras." Carnival is a time for parades, balls, and special parties. Everyone has so much fun dressing in formal clothes and beautiful costumes.

"We even have a Mardi Gras parade and ball in our school," said T-Boy as he laughed.

"And," added Lita, "we learn about the French people who brought the custom of Mardi Gras here when they settled New Orleans in the 1700s."

Jenny still wondered about the name and colors.

"You see, Jenny," interrupted Angelle, "the words *Mardi Gras* are French for 'Fat Tuesday.' That's the last day of the Carnival season.

"Also, the official colors are purple, green, and gold. Rex, the king of Carnival, picked those colors in the 1800s."

Jenny's eyes widened as she thought about how old the Mardi Gras customs were.

T-Boy then announced proudly that he knew the meanings of the Mardi Gras colors. "Purple means justice, green means faith, and gold means power."

Jenny was beginning to understand, but now she wanted to know more about the parades.

The children squealed with excitement as they thought about all the throws they would catch at the parades—pretty beads, toys, cups, doubloons, and so much more!

So, Jenny was told how a very long time ago, when parades started in New Orleans, men were the only people who paraded. They paid dues to belong to krewes or clubs, and they could be in the Carnival parade. However, as the years went on and Carnival customs grew, women and children wanted to start their own krewes, too.

Then Angelle held up a Mardi Gras-colored card. "We even have groups called super-krewes today, where anyone can join and be in a parade. And, Jenny, I think you are about to be part of one of these parades! Some friends will not be able to ride in their parade this year. So, they want to know if you and a guest would like to take their places on the float."

"Oh!" Lita exclaimed. "There are hundreds of riders in the super Krewe of Orpheus parade, with *so* many floats and lots of throws!"

Jenny was very thoughtful for a moment, then slowly she asked, "Do you think I could ask my mama to ride with me?"

Angelle and Claude smiled and nodded.

The next morning, Jenny could hardly eat her breakfast. Would she really see her mama today?

Since this was Jenny's first visit to the zoo, she closely followed Claude and Angelle. They were all greeted by friendly people at the entrance.

As they walked farther into the zoo, Jenny suddenly looked up. There, standing in her frontyard was Jenny's mother, smiling and waiting. Jenny felt that she could never be happier than at that moment.

Soon, everyone was talking excitedly about the upcoming parade. Then at the end of the visit, Lita asked, "Are we all going to the float preview party next weekend?"

"Most definitely!" exclaimed Jenny's mother.

The slight breeze coming off the Mississippi River made the floats seem alive as the colorful decorations danced in the wind.

As a jazz band played, people greeted each other, danced, took pictures, and walked around to find their names on their floats.

Finally Lita gasped. "There it is! It's tremendous!"

"That's right," said the float lieutenant as he greeted every-one. "Our Smokey Mary float is one of the largest floats ever built. It's so large that we'll even have our own jazz band on the top level. This will be just like the real Smokey Mary train that brought city people to the Lakefront many years ago."

At the end of the party, when everyone was leaving, Angelle mentioned that the next weekend would be a good time to go shopping for throws.

"Shopping? I have to buy my throws?" asked a surprised Jenny.

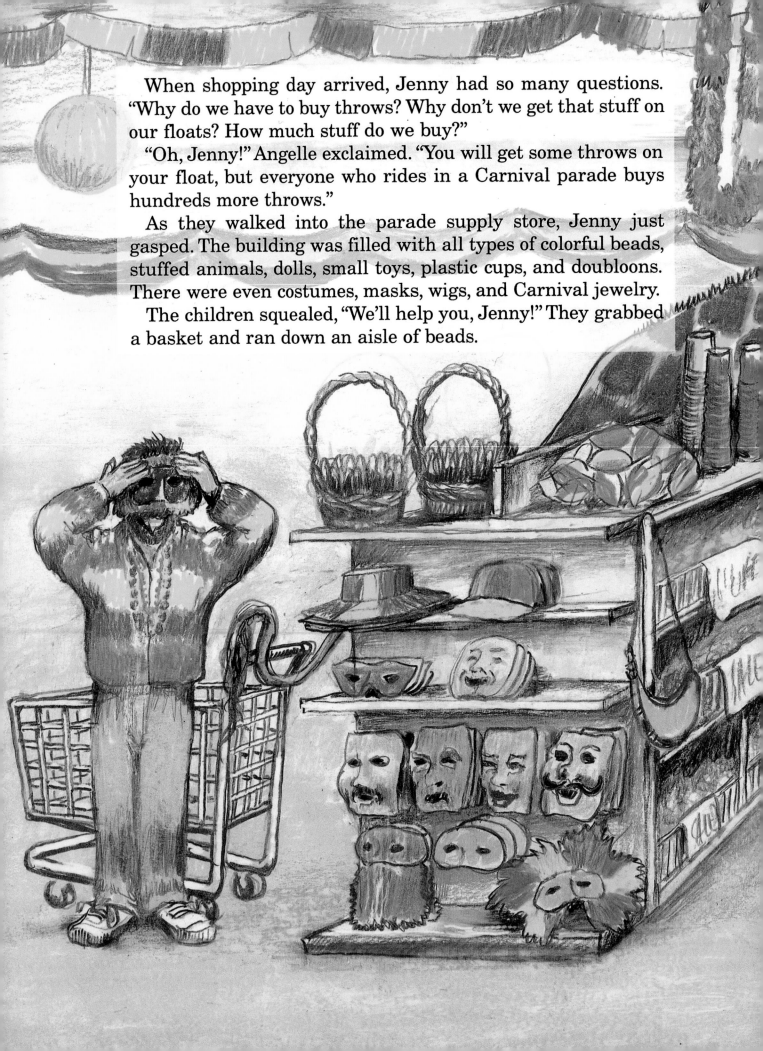

When shopping day arrived, Jenny had so many questions. "Why do we have to buy throws? Why don't we get that stuff on our floats? How much stuff do we buy?"

"Oh, Jenny!" Angelle exclaimed. "You will get some throws on your float, but everyone who rides in a Carnival parade buys hundreds more throws."

As they walked into the parade supply store, Jenny just gasped. The building was filled with all types of colorful beads, stuffed animals, dolls, small toys, plastic cups, and doubloons. There were even costumes, masks, wigs, and Carnival jewelry.

The children squealed, "We'll help you, Jenny!" They grabbed a basket and ran down an aisle of beads.

Jenny was so amazed as she picked up some beautiful long beads. "Do you mean that I'm going to buy these wonderful things and then throw them away?"

Angelle laughed. "No, they're not thrown away, they're thrown *to* people who come to see your parade. It's part of the Mardi Gras spirit. You're giving people the gifts of your parade."

"You see, Jenny," added Claude, "a parade is like a giant party, and people from our city and from all over the world come to your party. These are gifts for them to take home."

"I like that custom," Jenny thought as she started to shop.

The day of the Orpheus Super Parade finally arrived. The feeling of excitement was everywhere! The Convention Center area was extremely busy with all of the people, cars, and buses. The taxi was finally able to park close to the entrance so that everyone could help Jenny and her mother unload their parade throws.

There were empty boxes and bags everywhere!

"What fun this is going to be!" shouted T-Boy as he ran toward the float.

With so much help that morning, Jenny and her mother soon had all of their throws arranged. Short and long beads hung everywhere. Boxes of all types of throws, trinkets, toys, and games were stacked within easy reach.

There was much laughing and excitement as the float riders went to have lunch and then to be fitted for their costumes.

"Remember to look for us at the end of your parade Jenny!" yelled Lita as she was leaving. "And . . . throw us lots of stuff!"

Soon, everyone was dressed for the parade. Riders boarded the floats and attached themselves to their harnesses in case of a fall.

Now it was time for a long, slow ride to the beginning of the parade route.

As the ride began the float lieutenant reminded everyone, "Remember to keep on your harnesses, masks, hats, and costumes. If not, you may be taken off the float. Don't forget that our identities are supposed to be secret. And," he spoke slowly, "...we always throw stuff *to* people, not at them."

Soon the evening sky became dark, and the float lights began to flash almost magically.

Then the jazz bands, school bands, and military bands began to play. Jenny took a deep breath. Wouldn't you?

As the long float slowly turned the corner, it was cheered by thousands of voices. Jenny was so astounded by the tremendous number of people that she just stood there and stared.

"Throw, Jenny, throw!" called her mother excitedly. "They're all here to see our parade. Let's make sure they have fun!"

Jenny started throwing the beads first, then she threw cups, doubloons, and toys. Which ones would you have thrown first?

Many people on the parade route were clapping and dancing to the music of the jazz band. Some children were on ladders screaming, "Throw me something!" and reaching high for the colorful throws.

In fact, everyone seemed to be dancing, swaying, yelling, and catching throws.

After many blocks, one of the musicians shouted, "There's the Convention Center!" And the Smokey Mary float slowly followed the others into the building. The floats moved very slowly along the route between tables, chairs, and people. As the float Jenny was on finally entered the building, she was totally surprised. There, standing on tables and chairs and jumping and reaching for throws, were ladies in long dresses and men in tuxedos! "What a party!" she exclaimed and continued throwing.

Soon the floats were in their stopped positions along the wall.
And, as a group of second-line dancers passed by, Jenny and her
mother climbed down and joined in the festivities.

Friends and other family members were there. It was time for
the big inside party—time for more dancing and singing.

After a while, a very early breakfast was served . . . and the music continued.

Then, as with everything in life, the fun was coming to an end. People were leaving and carrying away their bags of throws.

The day after Mardi Gras, everyone was just a little tired. Fat Tuesday had been another fun-filled party day with even more parades and costumes. However, Jenny became very sad when her mother explained why she must return to her home in the zoo. "Now that Mardi Gras is over, it's time to go back to our normal lives."

"You see," her mother continued, "Mardi Gras is the last day of the Carnival season. We did party, eat, and drink as much as we wanted yesterday. But today is Ash Wednesday and now Lent begins."

"Lent?" questioned Jenny.

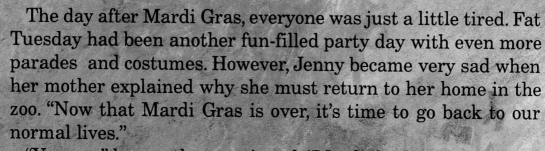

"Here we go again!" said Claude as he laughed. "Jenny has so much to discover."

"Lent is a time for fasting, and doing without some of the things that we like," he explained. "In that way we prepare for Easter."

"So, my dear Jenny," her mother went on, "we now return to our important jobs in life. I'll continue to help people learn about giraffes and," she said with a mother's pride, "you will help people enjoy our wonderful world with your paintings."

Jenny understood a little better, and she smiled thoughtfully. "Yes, and now that I finally know where you are, I can come visit you at any time."

"My first Mardi Gras is one that I will never forget. So many wonderful things have happened. I love you, Mama," said Jenny as she and her mother lovingly hugged each other.